Favorite Fairy Tales

~ Told In ~

ENGLAND

Retold from Joseph Jacobs

by Virginia Haviland

Illustrated by Maxie Chambliss

A Beech Tree Paperback Book
New York

10 9 8 7 6 5 4 3 2 1

These stories have been retold from *English Fairy Tales* collected by Joseph Jacobs (originally published 1892 by G.P. Putnam's sons).

Library of Congress Cataloging-in-Publication Data

Favorite fairy tales told in England / compiled by Virginia Haviland ;
    illustrated by Maxie Chambliss.
            p.   cm.
        "Retold from English fairy tales, collected by Joseph Jacobs
    (originally published 1892 by G.P. Putnam's Sons)"—
        Contents: Jack and the beanstalk — Johnny-cake — Tom Thumb —
    Molly Whuppie — Dick Whittington and his cat — Cap o' Rushes.
        ISBN 0-688-12595-6
        1. Fairy tales — England. [1. Fairy tales. 2. Folklore — England.]
    I. Haviland, Virginia, 1911-1988. II. Chambliss, Maxie, ill.   III. Jacobs, Joseph,
    1854-1916. English fairy tales.
    PZ8. F2794   1994
    398. 21' 0942 —dc20   93-29707
                                                                CIP
                                                                 AC

Minor editorial and style changes have been made in the stories for these new editions.

For Margery
My youngest reader
— V. H.

Contents

Jack and the Beanstalk

Jack and the Beanstalk

ONCE UPON A TIME there was a poor widow who had an only son named Jack and a cow named Milky-white. All they had to live on was the milk the cow gave every day. This they carried to the market and sold. But one morning Milky-white gave no milk.

"What shall we do? What shall we do?" cried the widow.

"Cheer up, Mother! I'll go and get work somewhere," said Jack.

"We've tried that before, and nobody would take you," said his mother. "We must sell Milky-white and with the money start a shop."

"All right, Mother," said Jack. "It's market day today. I'll soon sell Milky-white. Then we'll see what we can do."

So he took the cow's halter in his hand, and started off. He had not gone far when he met a funny-looking old man who said to him, "Good morning, Jack."

"Good morning to you," said Jack, wondering how the man knew his name.

"Well, Jack, and where are you off to?" said the man.

"I'm going to market to sell our cow."

"Oh, you look the proper sort of chap to sell cows," said the man. "I wonder if you know how many beans make five."

"Two in each hand and one in your mouth," said Jack, as sharp as a needle.

"Right you are," said the man, "and here they are, the very beans themselves." He pulled out of his pocket a number of strange-looking beans. "Since you are so sharp," said he, "I don't mind trading with you—your cow for these beans."

"Go along!" said Jack.

"Ah! You don't know what these beans are," said the man. "If you plant them at night, by morning the stalks will be right up to the sky."

"Really?" said Jack. "You don't say so."

"Yes, that is so, and if it doesn't turn out to be true you can have your cow back."

"Right," said Jack. He handed over Milky-white's halter and pocketed the beans.

Back home went Jack. It was not dusk by the time he got to his door.

"Back already, Jack?" said his mother. "I see you haven't got Milky-white, so you've sold her. How much did you get for her?"

"You'll never guess, Mother," said Jack.

"No, you don't say so! Good boy! Five pounds? Ten? Fifteen? No, it can't be twenty!"

"I told you you couldn't guess. What do you say to these beans? They're magical—plant them at night and…"

"What!" said Jack's mother. "Have you been such a fool as to give away my Milky-white for a set of dry beans? Take that! Take that! Take that!" and she gave him three hard slaps. "As for your magic beans, here they go out of the window. Now off with you to bed. Not a drop shall you drink, and not a bite shall you swallow this very night."

So Jack went upstairs to his little room in the attic. Sad and sorry he was, to be sure.

At last he dropped off to sleep.

When he woke up, his room looked very strange! The sun was shining, yet the room seemed dark and shadowy. Jack jumped up and ran to the window. What do you think he saw? Why, the beans his mother had thrown out of the window into the garden had sprung up into a big beanstalk. It went up and up and up till it reached the sky. The old man had spoken the truth after all.

The beanstalk grew close to Jack's window and ran up beyond like a great ladder. So Jack jumped onto the beanstalk and began to climb. He climbed, and he climbed, and he climbed, and he climbed, and he climbed, and he climbed, and he climbed. At last, through the clouds, he reached the sky. When he got there he found a long, broad road going on as straight as an arrow. So he walked along, and he walked along, and he walked along till he came to a great tall house. On the doorstep there was a great tall woman.

"Good morning, ma'm," said Jack, quite polite. "Could you be so kind as to give me some breakfast?" For he hadn't had anything to eat the night before, you know. He was as hungry as a hunter.

"It's breakfast you want, is it?" said the great tall woman. "It's breakfast you'll *be* if you don't move off from here. My man is a Giant, and there's nothing he likes better than boys broiled on toast. You'd better be moving on or he'll soon be coming."

"Oh! Please, ma'm, do give me something to eat, ma'm. I've had nothing since yesterday morning, really and truly, ma'm," said Jack. "I may as well be broiled as die of hunger."

Well, the Giant's wife was not half so bad after all. She took Jack into the kitchen, and gave him a chunk of bread and cheese and a jug of milk. But Jack hadn't half finished these when — *thump! thump! thump!* — the whole house began to tremble with the noise of someone coming.

"Goodness gracious me! It's my old man," said the Giant's wife. "What on earth shall I do? Come along quick and jump in here." She bundled Jack into the oven, just as the giant came in.

He was a big man, to be sure. At his belt he had

three calves strung up by the heels. He threw them down on the table and said, "Here, wife, broil me two of these for breakfast. Ah! What's this I smell?

> *Fee-fi-fo-fum,*
> *I smell the blood of an Englishman!*
> *Be he alive, or be he dead,*
> *I'll grind his bones to make my bread."*

"Nonsense, dear," said his wife. "You're dreaming. Or perhaps you smell the scraps of that little boy you liked so much for yesterday's dinner. Here, go wash and tidy up. By the time you come back, your breakfast will be ready for you."

Off the Giant went. Jack was just going to jump out of the oven and run away when the woman told him not to. "Wait till he's asleep," said she. "He always has a nap after breakfast."

The Giant had his breakfast. After that he went to a big chest and took out of it two bags of gold.

Down he sat and counted till at last his head began to nod. He began to snore till the whole house shook again.

Then Jack crept out on tiptoe from his oven. As he passed the Giant, he took one of the bags of gold under his arm. Off he ran till he came to the beanstalk. He threw down the bag of gold, which of course fell into his mother's garden. He climbed down and climbed down till at last he got home. He told his mother what had happened and showed her the gold.

"Well, Mother," he said, "wasn't I right about the beans? They *are* really magical, you see."

★ ★ ★

They lived on the bag of gold for some time, but at last they came to the end of it. Jack made up his mind to try his luck once more at the top of the beanstalk. So one fine morning he rose early and got onto the beanstalk. He climbed, and he

climbed, and he climbed, and he climbed, and he climbed, and he climbed. At last he came out onto the road again and up to the great tall house he had been to before. There, sure enough, was the great tall woman standing on the doorstep.

"Good morning, ma'm," said Jack, as bold as brass. "Could you be so good as to give me something to eat?"

"Go away, my boy," said the great tall woman, "or else my man will eat you up for breakfast. But aren't you the boy who came here once before? Do you know, that very day my man missed one of his bags of gold!"

"That's strange, ma'm," said Jack. "I dare say I could tell you something about that. But I'm so hungry I can't speak till I've had something to eat."

Well, the great tall woman was so curious that she took him in and gave him something to eat. But he had scarcely begun munching it, as slowly as he could, when — *thump! thump! thump!* — they heard the Giant's footsteps, and the wife again hid Jack in the oven.

Everything happened as before. In came the Giant, roaring *Fee-fi-fo-fum*, and he had a breakfast of three broiled oxen. Then he ordered, "Wife, bring me the hen that lays the golden eggs."

So she brought it. Her husband said, "Lay," and the hen laid an egg all of gold. But then the Giant began to nod his head, and to snore till the house shook.

Now Jack crept out of the oven on tiptoe and caught hold of the golden hen. He was off before you could say "Jack Robinson." This time, the Giant woke—because the hen gave a cackle. Just as Jack got out of the house, he heard the Giant calling, "Wife, Wife, what you have done with my golden hen?"

And the wife said, "Why, my dear?"

But that was all Jack heard, for he rushed off to the beanstalk and climbed down in a flash. When he got home he showed his mother the wonderful hen, and said "Lay!" to it. The hen laid a golden egg every time he said "Lay!"

★ ★ ★

Well, Jack was not content. It wasn't very long before he decided to try his luck again up there at the top of the beanstalk. One fine morning he rose early, and stepped onto the beanstalk. He climbed, and he climbed, and he climbed, and he climbed, till he came to the very top. This time he knew better than to go straight to the Giant's house. When he came near it, he waited behind a bush till he saw the Giant's wife come out with a pail to get some water. Then he crept into the house and hid in a copper tub. He hadn't been there long when he heard *thump! thump! thump!* as before. In walked the Giant and his wife.

"*Fee-fi-fo-fum*, I smell the blood of an English-man!" cried out the Giant. "I smell him, Wife, I smell him."

"Do you, my dear?" said his wife. "Well then, if it's the little rogue that stole your gold and the hen that laid the golden eggs, he's sure to have got into the oven." And they both rushed to the oven.

But Jack wasn't there, luckily. The Giant's wife said, "There you are again with your *Fee-fi-fo-fum*! Why, of course, it's the boy you caught last night that I've just broiled for your breakfast. How for-getful I am! And how careless you are not to know the difference between alive and dead, after all these years."

So the Giant sat down to his breakfast. Every now and then he would mutter, "Well I could have sworn...." And he'd get up and search the larder and the cupboards and everything. Only, luckily, he didn't think of the tub.

After breakfast, the Giant called out, "Wife, Wife,

bring me my golden harp." So she brought it and put it on the table before him. "Sing!" he ordered, and the golden harp sang most beautifully. It went on singing till the Giant fell asleep and began to snore like thunder.

Jack now got out of the tub very quietly and crept like a mouse over to the table. Up he crawled, caught hold of the golden harp, and dashed with it towards the door. But the harp called out quite loudly, "Master! Master!"

The Giant woke up just in time to see Jack running off with his harp.

Jack ran as fast as he could. The Giant came rushing after, and would soon have caught him, only Jack had a head start and knew where he was going. When he got to the beanstalk, the Giant was no more than twenty yards behind. Suddenly Jack disappeared. When the Giant came to the end of the road, he saw Jack below him climbing down for dear life.

Well, the Giant didn't like to trust himself to such a ladder. He stood and waited, so Jack got another lead.

But the harp cried out again, "Master! Master!" The Giant swung himself down onto the beanstalk, which shook with his weight. Down climbed Jack, and after him climbed the Giant.

Jack climbed down, and climbed down, and climbed down till he was very nearly home. Then he called out, "Mother! Mother! Bring me an ax, bring me an ax!" His mother rushed out with the ax in her hand. When she came to the beanstalk, she stood stock-still with fright. There was the Giant with his legs just through the clouds.

Jack jumped down, took the ax, and chopped at the beanstalk, almost cutting it in two. The Giant felt the beanstalk shake, so he stopped to see what was the matter. Then Jack chopped again. The beanstalk was cut in two. It began to topple over. Down crashed the Giant—and that was the end of him!

Jack gave his mother the golden harp. With the magical harp and the golden eggs, Jack and his mother became very rich. Jack married a Princess, and they all lived happily ever after.

Johnny - cake

Johnny - cake

NCE UPON A TIME there was an old man, and an old woman, and a little boy. One morning the old woman made a johnny-cake and put it in the oven to bake. "You watch the johnny-cake," she said to the little boy, "while your father and I go out to work in the garden."

The old man and the old woman went out and began to hoe potatoes, leaving the little boy to tend the oven. But he did not watch it all the time. Suddenly, when he was not watching, he heard a noise. He looked up and saw the oven door pop open. Out of the oven jumped Johnny-cake. He went rolling along end over end, towards the open door of the house.

The little boy ran to shut the door, but Johnny-cake was too quick for him. He rolled through the door, down the steps, and out into the road long before the little boy could catch him. The little boy ran after him as fast as he could run, crying out to his father and mother. They heard the uproar and threw down their hoes and chased Johnny-cake, too. But Johnny-cake outran all three and was soon out of sight. The little boy and his father and mother, out of breath, had to sit down on a bank to rest.

★   ★   ★

On ran Johnny-cake. By and by he came to two well-diggers. They looked up from their work and called out, "Where ye going, Johnny-cake?"

He said, "I've outrun an old man, and an old woman, and a little boy, and I can outrun you too-o-o!"

"Ye can, can ye? We'll see about that!" they cried. Then they threw down their picks and ran after him. But they couldn't catch up with him. Soon they had to sit down by the roadside to rest.

On ran Johnny-cake. By and by he came to two ditch-diggers, who were digging a ditch.

"Where ye going, Johnny-cake?" said they.

He said, "I've outrun an old man, and an old woman, and a little boy, and two well-diggers, and I can outrun you too-o-o!"

"Ye can, can ye? We'll see about that!" said they; and they threw down their spades and ran after him too. But Johnny-cake soon was way ahead of them, also. Seeing they could never catch him, they gave up the chase and sat down to rest.

On ran Johnny-cake, and by and by he came to a bear.

The bear said, "Where ye going, Johnny-cake?"

He said, "I've outrun an old man, and an old woman, and a little boy, and two well-diggers, and two ditch-diggers, and I can outrun you too-o-o!"

"Ye can, can ye?" snarled the bear. "We'll see about that!" He trotted as fast as his legs could carry him after Johnny-cake, who never stopped to look back. Before long the bear was left so far behind that he saw he might as well give up the

hunt first as last. He stretched himself out by the roadside to rest.

★ ★ ★

On ran Johnny-cake, and by and by he came to a wolf. The wolf said, "Where ye going, Johnny-cake?"

He said, "I've outrun an old man, and an old woman, and a little boy, and two well-diggers, and two ditch-diggers, and a bear, and I can outrun you too-o-o!"

"Ye can, can ye?" snarled the wolf. "We'll see about that!" And he set into a gallop after Johnny-cake, who went on and on so fast that the wolf saw there was no hope of overtaking him. He too lay down to rest.

★ ★ ★

On went Johnny-cake. By and by he came to a fox that lay quietly by the corner of a fence.

The fox called out in a sharp voice, but without getting up, "Where ye going, Johnny-cake?"

He said, "I've outrun an old man, and an old woman, and a little boy, and two well-diggers, and two ditch-diggers, and a bear, and a wolf, and I can outrun you too-o-o!"

The fox said, "I can't quite hear you, Johnny-

cake, won't you come a little closer?" as he turned his head a little to one side.

Johnny-cake stopped his race for the first time, and went a little closer. He called out in a very loud voice, *"I've outrun an old man, and an old woman, and a little boy, and two well-diggers, and two ditch-diggers, and a bear, and a wolf, and I can outrun you too-o-o!"*

"Can't quite hear you! Won't you come a *little* closer?" said the fox in a feeble voice. He stretched out his neck towards Johnny-cake, and put one paw behind his ear.

Johnny-cake came up close, and leaning towards the fox screamed out: "I'VE OUTRUN AN OLD MAN, AND AN OLD WOMAN, AND A LITTLE BOY, AND TWO WELL-DIGGERS, AND TWO DITCH-DIGGERS, AND A BEAR, AND A WOLF, AND I CAN OUTRUN YOU TOO-O-O!"

"You can, can you?" yelped the fox, and he snapped up Johnny-cake in his sharp teeth and ate him in the twinkling of an eye.

Tom Thumb

Tom Thumb

IN THE DAYS of the great King Arthur, there
lived a mighty magician called Merlin. He
was the most skillful wizard the world had
ever seen.

This famous magician, who could take any form
he pleased, was once traveling about as a beggar.
Being very tired, he stopped at a poor cottage to
rest, and asked for some food.

The countryman who lived there made him
welcome. The man's wife, who was a very kind

woman, brought him some milk in a wooden bowl and some coarse brown bread on a platter.

Merlin was much pleased. But he could not help seeing that the man and wife seemed unhappy, although everything was neat and snug in the cottage.

When Merlin asked them why they were so sad, the poor woman spoke with tears in her eyes. "It is because we have no children. I would be the happiest person in the world if I had a son. Even if he were no bigger than my husband's thumb, I would be satisfied."

Merlin was so amused by the idea of a boy the size of a man's thumb that he decided to grant the poor woman's wish. In a short time, the farmer's wife had a son. And he was not a bit bigger than his father's thumb!

One night while the mother was admiring the child, the Queen of the Fairies came in at the window. The Fairy Queen kissed the boy and named him Tom Thumb. She then sent for some of her fairies, who dressed him as she ordered:

A cap of oak-leaf for his crown;
A jacket woven of thistledown;
A shirt of web by spiders spun;
His trousers now of feathers done.
Stockings of apple-peel, to tie
With eyelash from his mother's eye;
Shoes made up of mouse's skin,
Tanned with the downy hair within.

Tom never grew any larger than his father's thumb, which was only of ordinary size. But as he grew older, he became very clever and full of tricks. When he was old enough to play marbles with the other boys, he sometimes lost all his marbles. Then he would creep into the bags of his playmates to refill his collection. Crawling out without being noticed, he would again join the game.

One day, as he was coming out of a bag of marbles, where he had been stealing as usual, the boy to whom the bag belonged saw him.

"Aha! my little Tommy," said the boy, "so at last I have caught you stealing my marbles. You shall be punished for your trick."

He drew the string of the bag tight around Tom's neck and gave the bag such a shake that poor little Tom was in great pain. He cried out and begged to be let free. "I will never steal again!" he said.

A short time later his mother was making a batter pudding. Tom, being anxious to see how it was made, climbed up to the edge of the bowl. Then his foot slipped and he fell into the batter. His mother had not seen him. She stirred him into the pudding, and put it in the pot to boil.

The batter filled Tom's mouth and prevented him from crying. But he kicked and struggled so much as the pot grew hot that his mother thought the pudding was bewitched. Taking it out of the pot, she threw it outside the door. A poor tinker who was passing by picked up the pudding, slipped it into his bag, and walked off with it.

By now Tom had got his mouth cleared of the batter, and he began to cry aloud. This frightened the tinker so much that he flung down the pudding and ran away. The pudding string broke. Tom crept out covered all over with batter, and walked home. His mother was very sorry to see her darling in such a state. She put him into a teacup and washed off the batter. Then she kissed him, and laid him in bed.

★ ★ ★

Soon after this, Tom's mother went to milk her cow in the meadow and took Tom along with her. Lest the high wind should blow him away, she tied him to a thistle with a piece of fine thread. But the cow saw Tom's oak leaf hat. She liked the looks of it and grabbed poor Tom and the thistle in one mouthful.

Tom was afraid of her great teeth and roared out as loud as he could, "Mother, Mother!"

"Where are you, Tommy?" asked his mother.

"Here, Mother, in the red cow's mouth."

His mother began to cry. But the cow, surprised at the odd noise Tom was making in her throat, opened her mouth and let Tom drop out. Luckily his mother caught him in her apron as he was falling down, or he would have been dreadfully hurt.

★ ★ ★

One day Tom's father made him a whip out of barley straw so that he could drive the cattle. Out in the field Tom slipped. He rolled over and over into a steep furrow of earth. A raven, flying over, picked him up and carried him out to sea. There it dropped him.

The moment Tom fell into the sea, a large fish swallowed him. Soon after, this very fish was

caught, and was bought for the table of King Arthur. When the cook opened the fish in order to cook it, out jumped the tiny boy!

Tom was happy to be free again. The cook carried him to the King, who made Tom his special dwarf. Soon he grew to be a great favorite at court. By his tricks and fun, he amused the King and Queen, and also all the Knights of the Round Table.

The King quite often took Tom with him when he rode out on his horse. If it rained, Tom would creep into the King's pocket and sleep till the rain was over.

One day King Arthur asked Tom about his parents. The King wished to know if they were as small as Tom and whether they were well off. Tom told the King that his father and mother were as tall as anyone about the court, but rather poor. The King then carried Tom to the room where he kept all his money and told him to take as much as he could carry home to his parents. Tom, full of joy, at once got a purse. But it would hold only one silver piece. Even this he could hardly lift.

At last he managed to place this load on his back, and he set off for his journey home. After resting more than a hundred times by the way, he reached his father's house in two days and two nights.

Tom was tired almost to death. His mother carried him into the house.

★　★　★

During his visit Tom told his parents many stories about the court. Then one day, he decided he must return to the King.

Back at the court, the King noticed how much Tom's clothes had suffered from being in the batter pudding and inside the fish, as well as from his journey. So the King ordered a new suit made for him. And he had Tom mounted on a mouse, like a knight, with a needle for a sword.

It was great fun to see Tom in his new suit, mounted on the mouse. When he rode out hunting with the King and his knights, everyone was ready to laugh.

The King was so pleased with Tom that he also had a little chair made, so that Tom might sit upon his table. Then to live in he gave him a little palace of gold, with a door an inch wide. There was a coach, too, drawn by six small mice.

In this way Tom was happy for a long time, and his parents were pleased with his success.

Molly Whuppie

Molly Whuppie

ONCE UPON A TIME a man and his wife had too many children. They could not feed them all, so they took the three youngest and left them in a wood. The three little girls walked and walked, but never a house could they see. It began to be dark, and they were hungry.

At last the little girls saw a light and headed in that direction. The light shone from a house. They rapped on the door, and a woman came who said, "What do you want?"

"Please let us in and give us something to eat."

The woman answered, "I can't do that, as my husband is a Giant. He would kill you when he comes home."

"Do let us stop for a little while," they begged, "and we will go away before he comes."

The woman took them in. She let them sit by the fire and gave them bread and milk.

Just as they began to eat, a great knock came to the door, and a dreadful voice said: *"Fee-Fi-Fo-Fum, I smell the blood of some earthly one*—Who's there, Wife?"

"Eh," said the wife, "it's three poor lassies, cold and hungry. They'll go away. Ye won't touch 'em, Man."

The Giant said nothing. He ate up a big supper, and ordered the girls to stay all night. He had three lassies of his own, he said, who would sleep in the same bed as the three strangers.

Now the youngest of the three girls was called

Molly Whuppie, and she was very clever. She noticed that before they went to bed the Giant put straw ropes round her neck and the necks of her sisters. Around his own daughters' necks he put gold chains. So Molly took care not to fall asleep, and waited till she was sure everyone was sleeping soundly.

Then Molly slipped out of bed. She took the straw ropes off her own and her sisters' necks, and took the gold chains off the Giant's lassies. She then put the straw ropes on the Giant's daughters and the gold ones on herself and her sisters, and lay down.

In the middle of the night up rose the Giant, and he felt for the necks with the straw. It was dark. He took his own daughters out of bed, and carried them out to a cage where he locked them up. Then he lay down again.

Molly thought it was time she and her sisters were off and away. She woke them and told them to be quiet, and they slipped out of the house. They all got out safe, and they ran and ran.

★ ★ ★

They never stopped until morning, when they saw a grand house before them.

It turned out to be a King's house, so Molly went in and told her story to the King. The King said, "Well, Molly, you are a clever girl. You have managed well. But—you can manage better yet. Go back and steal the Giant's sword that hangs over his bed, and I'll give your eldest sister my eldest son to marry."

Molly said she would try. So she went back. She managed to slip into the Giant's house and to hide under his bed.

The Giant came home, ate up a great supper, and went to bed. Molly waited until he was snoring. Then she crept out and reached over the giant and got down the sword. But just as she got it out

over the bed, the sword gave a rattle. Up jumped the Giant!

Molly ran out the door, carrying the sword with her. She ran, and the Giant ran, till they came to the Bridge of One Hair. She got over, but he couldn't; and he cried, "Woe unto ye, Molly Whuppie, if ye ever come here again!"

But Molly replied, "Twice yet I'll come to Spain."

So Molly took the sword to the King, and her sister was wed to his son.

And the King said, "You've managed well, Molly. But you can do better yet. Go back and steal the purse that lies beneath the giant's pillow, and I'll marry your second sister to my second son."

Molly said she would try. So she set out for the Giant's house and slipped in and hid again under his bed. She waited till the Giant had eaten his supper and was sound asleep snoring.

She crept out then. She slipped her hand under the pillow, and got the purse. But just as she was leaving, the giant woke up and ran after her.

She ran, and he ran, till they came to the Bridge of One Hair. She got over, but he couldn't; and he cried, "Woe unto ye, Molly Whuppie, if ye ever come here again!"

But Molly replied, "Once yet I'll come to Spain."

So Molly took the purse to the King, and her second sister was wed to the King's second son.

After that the King said to Molly, "Molly, you are a clever girl. But you can do better yet. Steal the Giant's ring that he wears on his finger, and I'll give you my youngest son for yourself."

Molly said she would try. So back she went to the Giant's house and hid under the bed. The Giant wasn't long in coming home. After he had eaten a great supper, he went to his bed, and shortly was snoring loud.

Molly crept out and reached over the bed. She took hold of the Giant's hand. She pulled and she pulled at the ring on his finger. But just as she got it off, the Giant rose up and gripped her by the hand. "Now I have caught ye, Molly Whuppie! Well, now—if I had done as much ill to ye as ye have done to me, what would ye do to me?"

At once Molly said, "I would put you into a sack. I'd put the cat inside with you, and the dog beside you, and a needle and thread and shears. And I'd hang you up on the wall. Then I'd go to the wood, and I would choose the biggest stick I could get. I would come home and take you down and bang you till you were dead."

"Well, Molly," said the Giant, "I'll do just that to ye."

So he got a sack, and put Molly into it, with the cat and the dog beside her, and a needle and thread and shears. He hung her up on the wall. Then he went to the wood to choose a stick.

Molly sang out, "Oh, if you saw what I see!"

"Oh," said the Giant's wife, "what do you see, Molly?"

But Molly never said a word, only, "Oh, if you saw what I see!"

The Giant's wife begged Molly to take her up into the sack so she could see what Molly saw. So Molly took the shears and cut a hole in the sack. She took the needle and thread out with her, and jumped down and helped the Giant's wife up into the sack, and sewed up the hole. The Giant's wife saw nothing, and began to ask to get down again. But Molly never minded. She hid herself behind the door. Home came the giant with a big tree in his hand. He took down the sack and began to batter it. His wife cried out, "It's me, Man, it's me!" But the dog barked so, and the cat mewed so, that the Giant did not hear his wife's voice.

Molly came out from behind the door. The Giant saw her and ran after her. He ran, and she ran, till they came to the Bridge of One Hair. She got over, but he couldn't; and he said, "Woe unto ye, Molly Whuppie, if ye ever come here again!"

But Molly replied, "Never more will I come to Spain."

So Molly took the ring to the King. She was married to his youngest son, and she never saw the Giant again.

Dick Whittington
and His Cat

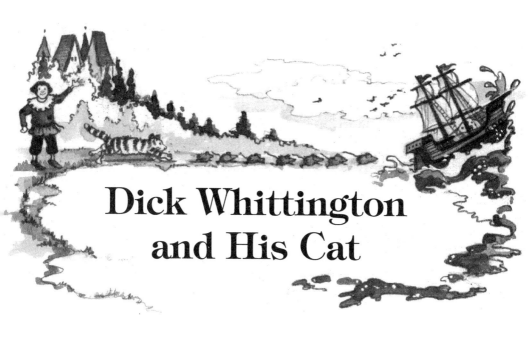

Dick Whittington
and His Cat

MANY YEARS AGO there lived a little boy whose name was Dick Whittington. Dick's father and mother died when he was very young. As he was not old enough to work, he was very badly off. The people who lived in his village were so poor that they could give him little more than the parings of potatoes, and sometimes a hard crust of bread.

Dick had heard many strange things about the great city called London. The country people thought that folks there were all fine gentlemen and ladies. They believed that singing and music were heard all day long and the streets were paved with gold.

★ ★ ★

Time passed till one day a wagoner was driving a large wagon through Dick's village on his way to London. Dick asked if he might walk with him by the side of the wagon. When the man learned that poor Dick had no father or mother, and saw by his ragged clothes that he could be no worse off than he was already, he told him he might go. So they set off together.

Dick got safely to London and ran off as fast as he could to look for the streets paved with gold. He ran until he was tired. At last, when it was dark and he had found every street covered with dirt instead of gold, he sat down in a corner and cried himself to sleep.

The next morning he got up and walked about, asking everybody he met to give him a coin to keep him from starving. Only two or three people gave him money, and he was soon weak from hunger.

At length Dick laid himself down at the door of Mr. Fitzwarren, a rich merchant. Here he was found by the cook, who had a very nasty temper. She was busy getting dinner for her master and mistress, so she called out to poor Dick, "What business have you here, you lazy boy? If you do not take yourself away, we'll see how you'll like a sousing of dishwater. I have some hot enough to make you jump!"

Just then Mr. Fitzwarren himself came home to dinner. When he saw the dirty ragged boy lying at the door, he said to him, "Why do you lie here, my boy? You seem old enough to work. I am afraid you are lazy."

"No, indeed, sir," said Dick. "I would gladly work, but I don't know anybody, and I'm sick for lack of food."

"Poor boy, get up. Let me see what ails you."

Dick tried to rise, but had to lie down again, for he had not eaten in three days. The kind merchant then ordered him to be taken into the house and given a good dinner. He was to stay, to do what work he could for the cook.

★ ★ ★

Dick would have lived very happily with this good family if it had not been for the ill-natured cook. She would scold him and beat him cruelly with a broom. At last her bad treatment was reported to Alice, Mr. Fitzwarren's daughter, who told the woman she would be turned away if she did not treat Dick more kindly.

The cook's behavior became a little better, but Dick suffered another hardship. His bed stood in a garret, where there were so many holes in the floor and walls that every night rats and mice ran over him. One day when he had earned a penny for cleaning a gentleman's shoes, he thought he would buy a cat with it.

He saw a girl with a cat, so he asked her, "Will you let me have that cat for a penny?"

The girl said "Yes, that I will, and she is an excellent mouser."

Dick hid his cat in the garret, and always took care to take part of his dinner to her. In a short

time he had no more trouble with rats and mice, but slept soundly every night.

Soon after this, one of Mr. Fitzwarren's trading ships was ready to sail. It was the custom for all his servants to share in the profits of a voyage, so he called them into the parlor and asked them what they would send out to trade.

They all had something that they were willing to send, except poor Dick. For this reason he did not come into the parlor with the rest. But Miss Alice guessed what was the matter and ordered him to be called in. "I will lay down some money for him, from my own purse," she said.

But her father told her, "This will not do. It must be something of his own."

When poor Dick heard this, he said, "I have nothing but a cat which I once bought for a penny."

"Fetch your cat, then, my lad," said Mr. Fitzwarren, "and let her go."

Dick went upstairs. With tears in his eyes, he

brought down poor Puss. Giving her to the ship's captain, he thought, "Now again I'll be kept awake all night by rats and mice." But Miss Alice, who felt pity for him, gave him money to buy another cat.

This kindness shown by Miss Alice made the cook jealous of poor Dick. She began to treat him more cruelly than ever, and always made fun of him for sending his cat to sea.

At last poor Dick could bear it no longer. He thought he would run away. So he packed up his few things and started off, very early. He walked as far as Holloway, and there sat down on a stone to think about which road he should take.

While he was considering this, the bells of Bow Church began to ring, and seemed to say to him:

Turn again, Whittington,
Thrice Lord Mayor of London.

"Lord Mayor of London!" said Dick to himself. "Why, to be sure, I'd put up with almost anything now—to be Lord Mayor of London, and ride in a fine coach, when I grow to be a man! Well, I will go back. I'll think nothing of the cuffing and scolding, if I'm to be Lord Mayor of London."

Dick did go back and was lucky enough to get into the house and set about his work before the cook came downstairs.

★ ★ ★

Now we must follow Puss to the coast of Africa. The ship, with the cat on board, was a long time at sea. At last it was driven by the winds to a part of the coast of Barbary. The Moors who lived there came in great numbers to see the sailors, and treated them politely. After they became better acquainted, the Moors were eager to buy the fine things that the ship carried.

When the captain saw this, he sent examples of the best things he had to the King of the country.

The King was so pleased that he invited the captain to come to the palace. Here they all sat on carpets woven with gold and silver, as was the custom. Rich dishes were brought in for dinner. However, a vast number of rats and mice rushed in too. These ate all the meat in an instant!

The captain learned that the King would give half his treasure to be freed of the rats and mice. "They not only destroy his dinner," the captain was told, "but they attack him in his chamber, and even in bed. He has to be watched while he is sleeping."

The captain was delighted! He remembered poor Whittington and his cat, and told the King that he had an animal on board ship that would do away with all these pests at once. The King jumped so high for joy that his turban dropped off his head.

"Bring this animal at once," he said. "Rats and

mice are dreadful! If she will do as you say, I will load your ship with gold and jewels in exchange for her!"

Cleverly, the captain set forth the merits of Puss. He told the King, "It is not very convenient to part with her, for, when she is gone, the rats and mice may destroy the goods in the ship. But to oblige Your Majesty, I will fetch her."

"Run, run!" said the Queen. "I'm impatient to see the dear creature."

Away went the captain to the ship, while another dinner was made ready. He put Puss under his arm, and arrived at the palace just in time to see the table again covered with rats. When the cat saw them, she did not wait for orders, but jumped out of the captain's arms. In a few minutes almost all of the rats and mice were dead at her feet. The rest of them scampered away to their holes in fright.

The King was happy to get rid of the plague so easily. He was pleased, too, to learn that Puss's

kittens would keep the whole country free from rats. So he gave the captain ten times as much for the cat as for all the rest of the cargo.

The captain now could take leave of the court and set sail for England.

★ ★ ★

Early one morning Mr. Fitzwarren had just sat

down to his countinghouse desk, when he heard
somebody—*tap, tap*—at his door.

"Who's there?" said Mr. Fitzwarren.

"A friend," answered the other. "I come to bring
you good news of your ship, the *Unicorn*."

The merchant opened his door. Whom should
he see waiting but his captain and his agent with a
cabinet of jewels! He looked at their report of the
trading, and thanked Heaven for giving him such
a prosperous voyage.

He heard the story of the cat and saw the rich
gifts that the King and Queen had sent to poor
Dick. He called out to his servants, "Go send him
in, and tell him of his fame; pray call him Mr.
Whittington by name."

Mr. Fitzwarren proved he was a good man. Some
of his servants said that so great a treasure was too
much for Dick. He answered them, "God forbid I
should deprive him of the value of a single penny."

Dick was at that time scouring pots for the cook,

and quite dirty. He wanted to excuse himself from coming into the countinghouse, but the merchant ordered him to enter.

Mr. Fitzwarren had a chair set for him. Dick began to think they were making fun of him and said, "Don't play tricks with me. Let me go back to my work, if you please."

"Indeed, Mr. Whittington," said the merchant, "we are all quite in earnest. I rejoice in the news that these gentlemen have brought you. The captain has sold your cat to the King of Barbary. In return for her you have more riches than I possess in the whole world. I wish you may long enjoy them!"

Poor Dick was so full of joy that he hardly knew how to behave. He begged his master to take any part of the treasure that he pleased, since he owed it all to his kindness.

"No, no," answered Mr. Fitzwarren, "this is all yours. I know you will use it well."

Dick next asked his mistress, and then Miss Alice, to accept a part of his good fortune. But they would not. Dick was too generous to keep it all to himself, however. He gave presents to the captain, the agent, and the rest of Mr. Fitzwarren's servants—even to the ill-natured old cook.

After this, Mr. Fitzwarren advised Dick to send for a tailor and have himself dressed like a gentleman. He told him he was welcome to live in his house till he could provide himself with a better one.

When Whittington's face was washed, his hair curled, his hat cocked, and he was dressed in a fine suit of clothes, he was as handsome as any young gentleman who visited at Mr. Fitzwarren's. Miss Alice, who had once been so kind to him and thought of him with pity, now looked upon him as fit to be her sweetheart. Whittington thought always of how to please her, and gave her the prettiest gifts he could find.

Mr. Fitzwarren soon saw that they loved each other, and proposed to join them in marriage. To this they both readily agreed. Their wedding was attended by the Lord Mayor, the court of aldermen, the sheriffs, and a great number of the richest merchants in London.

★ ★ ★

Mr. Whittington and his lady lived on in great splendor and were very happy, with several children. He became Sheriff of London and thrice Lord Mayor, and from the King he received the honor of knighthood. Each time he became Lord Mayor, he recalled the sound of Bow Bells:

Turn again, Whittington,
Thrice Lord Mayor of London.

Cap o' Rushes

Cap o' Rushes

ONCE UPON A TIME there was a very rich gentleman who had three beautiful daughters. He thought he would see how fond they were of him.

He asked the first, "How much do you love me, my dear?"

"Why," said she, "as I love my life."

"That's good," he replied.

He then asked the second, "How much do *you* love me, my dear?"

"Why, better than all the world," said she.

"That's good," he answered.

He turned then to the third, who was clever as well as pretty.

"How much do *you* love me, my dear?"

"Why, I love you as fresh meat loves salt!"

My, but he was angry! "You don't love me at all," he said, "and in my house you shall stay no longer." So he drove her out there and then, and slammed the door after her.

She went away, on and on till she came to a swamp. In that low, marshy place she gathered some rushes and wove them into a kind of cloak with a hood, to cover her from head to foot and hide her fine clothes. Then she went on and on till she came to a great house.

"Do you need a maid?" she asked.

"No, we don't," they said.

"I have nowhere to go," she said, "and I ask no wages. I'll do any sort of work."

"Well," they said, "if you like to wash pots and scrape pans you may stay."

So she stayed, and she washed the pots and scraped the pans and did all the dirty work. Because she did not tell them her name, they called her Cap o' Rushes.

One day there was to be a great dance nearby. The servants were allowed to go and look on at the grand people. Cap o' Rushes said she was too tired to go, so she stayed home.

When they were gone, she took off her cap o' rushes and cleaned herself. And away she went to the dance, for she loved to dance. No one could dance more beautifully. And no one there was so finely dressed as she.

Now who should be there but her master's son! And what should he do but fall in love with her the minute he set eyes on her! He refused to dance with anyone else.

But before the dance was done, Cap o' Rushes slipped away home.

When the other maids came back, she was pretending to be asleep with her cap o' rushes on.

★ ★ ★

Next morning they said to her, "You did miss a sight, Cap o' Rushes!"

"What was that?" she said.

"Why, the most beautiful lady you ever did see, dressed right rich and gay. The young master, he never took his eyes off her."

"Well, I should like to have seen her," said Cap o' Rushes.

"There's to be another dance this evening; perhaps she'll be there."

But when evening came, Cap o' Rushes said she was too tired to go with them. Still, she remembered the young master, who danced so well. When the others had gone, she took off her cap o' rushes and cleaned herself. And away she went to the dance.

The master's son had counted on seeing her. He danced with no one else, and never took his eyes off her. But before the dance was over, she slipped away, and home she went. When the maids came back she pretended to be asleep with her cap o' rushes on.

★ ★ ★

Next day they said to her again, "Well, Cap o' Rushes, you should have been there to see the lady! There she was again, right rich and gay. The young master, he never took his eyes off her."

"Well, there," she said, "I should like to have seen her."

"Good," they said, "there's another dance this evening. You must go with us, for she's sure to be there."

Well, at evening Cap o' Rushes again said she was too tired to go. But when the maids were gone, she took off her cap o' rushes and cleaned herself. And away she went to the dance.

The master's son was full of joy to see her. He danced with no one else and never took his eyes off her. When she wouldn't tell him her name, nor where she came from, he gave her a ring. He told her that if he didn't see her again he would die.

Well, before the dance was over, she slipped away, and home she went. When the maids came home she was pretending to be asleep with her cap o' rushes on.

Next day they said to her, "There, Cap o' Rushes, you didn't come last night. Now you won't see the lady, for there's no more dances."

"I should like to have seen her," said Cap o' Rushes.

The master's son tried every way to find out where the lady had gone. But go where he might, and ask whom he might, he never heard anything about her. And he felt worse and worse for love of her till he was so ill he had to take to his bed.

★ ★ ★

"Make some gruel for the young master," everyone said to the cook. "He's dying for the love of the lady." The cook set about making it when Cap o' Rushes came in.

"What are you doing?" she asked.

"I'm going to make some gruel for the young master," said the cook, "for he's dying for the love of the lady."

"Let me make it," said Cap o' Rushes.

Well, the cook wouldn't allow her at first. But at last she said yes, and Cap o' Rushes made the gruel. When she had made it, she slipped the ring into it before the cook took it upstairs.

The young man drank it. Then he saw the ring at the bottom.

"Send for the cook," he said.

So up she came.

"Who made this gruel?" he asked.

"I did," said the cook, for she was frightened.

"No, you didn't," he said. "Say who did it, and you shan't be harmed."

"Well, then, 'twas Cap o' Rushes."

"Send Cap o' Rushes here," he said.

Cap o' Rushes came.

"Did you make my gruel?" he asked.

"Yes, I did," she replied.

"Where did you get this ring?"

"From him that gave it to me," she answered.

"Who are you, then?" asked the young man.

"I'll show you," she said. And she took off her cap o' rushes, and there she was in her beautiful clothes.

Well, the master's son—he got well very soon. And they were to be married in a short time. It was to be a grand wedding, with everyone invited from far and near. Cap o' Rushes' father was invited, too, but his daughter never told anybody who she was.

★ ★ ★

Before the wedding, Cap o' Rushes went to the cook and said, "I want you to prepare every dish without a mite of salt."

"That'll be plain nasty," said the cook.

"That doesn't matter," she replied.

"Very well," said the cook.

★ ★ ★

The wedding day came, and they were married. And after they were married, all the company sat down at the feast. When they began to chew the meat, it was so tasteless they couldn't eat it. Cap o' Rushes's father tried first one dish and then another. Then he burst out crying.

"What's the matter?" asked the master's son.

"Oh!" he said, "I had a daughter, whom I loved very much. When I asked her how much she loved me, she said, 'As much as fresh meat loves salt.' I turned her away from my door, for I thought she didn't love me. Now I see that she loved me best of all. And she may be dead, for all I know."

"No, Father, here she is!" said Cap o' Rushes. And she went up to him and put her arms around him.

And so they were happy ever after.

About This Series

IN RECENT DECADES, folk tales and fairy tales from all corners of the earth have been made available in a variety of handsome collections and in lavishly illustrated picture books. But in the 1950s, such a rich selection was not yet available. The classic fairy and folk tales were most often found in cumbersome books with small print and few illustrations. Helen Jones, then children's book editor at Little, Brown and Company, accepted a proposal from a Boston librarian for an ambitious series with a simple goal — to put an international selection of stories into the hands of children. The tales would be published in slim volumes, with wide margins and ample leading, and illustrated by a cast of contemporary artists. The result was a unique series of books intended for children to read by themselves — the Favorite Fairy Tales series. Available only in hardcover for many years, the books have now been reissued in paperbacks that feature new illustrations and covers.

The series embraces the stories of sixteen different countries: Czechoslovakia, Denmark, England, India,

France, Italy, Ireland, Germany, Greece, Japan, Scotland, Norway, Poland, Sweden, Spain, and Russia. Some of these stories may seem violent or fantastical to our modern sensibilities, yet they often reflect the deepest yearnings and imaginings of the human mind and heart.

Virginia Haviland traveled abroad frequently and was able to draw on librarians, storytellers, and writers in countries as far away as Japan to help make her selections. But she was also an avid researcher with a keen interest in rare books, and most of the stories she included in the series were found through a diligent search of old collections. Ms. Haviland was associated with the Boston Public Library for nearly thirty years — as a children's and branch librarian, and eventually as Readers Advisor to Children. She reviewed for *The Horn Book Magazine* for almost thirty years and in 1963 was named Head of the Children's Book Section of the Library of Congress. Ms. Haviland remained with the Library of Congress for nearly twenty years, and wrote and lectured about children's literature throughout her career. She died in 1988.